Little
Mermaid

This book belongs to:

....

make
believe
ideas

Little
Mermaid

Key sounds: s, m, u
Secondary sound: ng

Written by Lucy Waterhouse
Illustrated by Clare Fennell

How to use this book

The **Reading with Phonics** series helps you to have fun with your child and to support their learning of phonics and reading. It is aimed at children who have learnt the letter sounds and are now ready to practise what they have learnt.

Each title in the series focuses on three key sounds. The enjoyable retelling of the story repeats these sounds frequently, and they are highlighted in bold type. The first activity at the back of the book provides practice in reading and using words containing these sounds. The key sounds for **The Little Mermaid** are /s/, /m/ and /u/, represented by the letters **s**, **m** and **u**.

Start by reading the story to your child, asking them to join in with the refrain. Next, encourage them to read the story with you. Help them decode tricky words.

Now look at the activity pages at the back of the book. These are intended for you and your child to enjoy together. Most are not activities to complete in pencil or pen, but by reading and talking or pointing.

The **key sound** pages focus on the three key sounds in the story. Help your child to read the words and trace the route on the word maps.

The **secondary sound** pages look at a pair of letters and at the sound they make as they work together. Encourage your child to read the words and complete the activity so they become more comfortable with the sound.

Rhyme is used in these retellings. Whatever stage your child has reached in their learning of phonics, it is always good practice to listen carefully for sounds and find words that rhyme. The pages on **rhyming words** take six words from the story and ask children to read and find other words that rhyme with them.

The **sight words** pages focus on a number of words that occur frequently but can still be challenging. Many of these words are not sounded out following the rules of phonics, and it's best for children to learn them by sight as this will improve their fluency. These pages encourage children to retell the story, practising sight words as they do so.

The **picture dictionary** page asks children to focus closely on nine words from the story. Encourage children to look carefully at each word, cover it with a hand, write it on a separate piece of paper, and finally, check it.

Do not complete all the activities at once – doing one each time you read will ensure that your child continues to enjoy the stories and the time you are spending together. **Have fun!**

One **morning**
in the ocean,
Mermaid **Su**nshine
heard a shout.

A boat was **s**inki**ng** in the waves. **So**meone could not get out.

Sunshine loved to **sing** all day.
Swimmi**ng** **m**ade her lo**ng** tail **s**way.

Sunshine swam
towards the boat
and found a
prince asleep.

She used her voice
to wake him up
then swam off
to the deep.

Sunshine loved to **sing** all day.
She **s**aved the **m**an then **s**wam away.

Sunshine's head
was in a daze.
"The prince seems great,"
she said.

"He'd never love
my tail, though.
Maybe **M**eg could
give **m**e legs."

Sunshine loved to **sing** all day.
Maybe Meg would find the way.

Magic Meg
made potions
from strange stuff
in the sea.

She **s**aid she would
help **Su**nshine
if she could pay
her fee.

Sunshine loved to **sing** all day.
Meg thought **up** a fee to pay.

Sunshine told Meg
her one true wish:
"I **mu**st have
human legs."

"If you **sing**
into this shell,
I'll grant your wish,"
said Meg.

Sunshine loved to **sing** all day,
but Meg stole Sunshine's voice away.

Soon, **Su**nshine had
two new legs
and **s**kipped
alo**ng** the shore.

Prince **S**am
started calli**ng**:
"Have I **m**et
you before?"

Sunshine loved to **sing** all day.
The handsome prince chose to **s**tay.

Sunshine joined Sam
on his boat.
He leaned in
for a kiss.

Sunshine thought,
"I have no voice.
How can I talk
like this?"

Sunshine used to **sing** all day.
There was nothi**ng** she could **s**ay.

Meg was watching
from the sea.
"Join me, Sam!"
she sang.

Meg had stolen
Sunshine's voice
and now wanted
her man.

Sunshine used to sing all day.
Magic Meg made Sam obey.

The shell with
Sunshine's voice inside
was on a
nearby rock.

A **s**eagull pecked
the shell in two,
and **M**eg cried out
in shock.

Sunshine loved to **sing** all day.
Her **singing** voice was back, hooray!

Magic Meg
was forced to leave,
and **S**am and **Su**nshine
were wed.

Sunshine's wishes
had come true,
no thanks to
mean old Meg.

Sunshine loved to sing all day.
Meg was sent off far away.

Key sounds

Look at these letters and say the sounds they make.

s   **m**   **u**

Follow the words that start with **s** to reach **Sam**.

| s | sing | boat |

waves — swam

saved — bird

rock — sea

Sam — deal

Follow the words that start with **m** to reach the **m**ermaids.

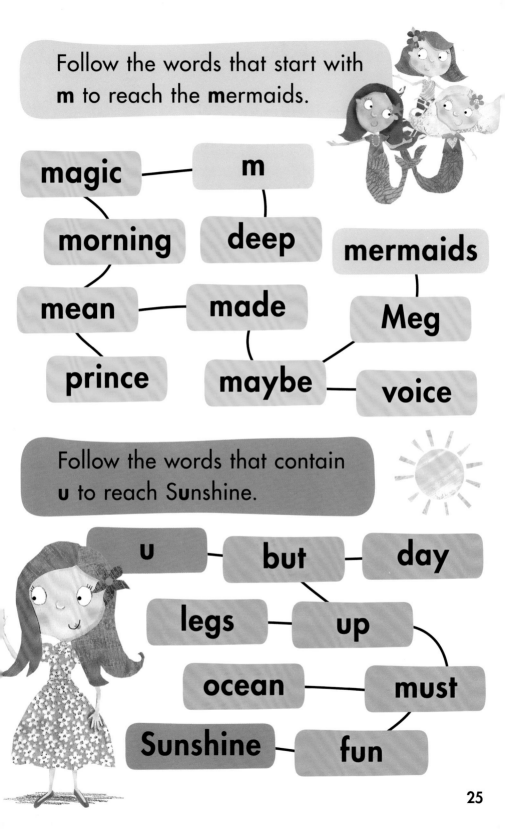

magic — m

morning — deep — mermaids

mean — made — Meg

prince — maybe — voice

Follow the words that contain **u** to reach S**u**nshine.

u — but — day

legs — up

ocean — must

Sunshine — fun

25

Secondary sound

Together, the letters **n** and **g** have a voiced nasal sound. This sound often comes at the end of a word. Find each word with the **ng** sound, then use it in a sentence.

morning
shout

long
sinking

sing
tail

swimming
daze

singing
kiss

potions
watching

wish
sang

Rhyming words

Read and say the words in the flowers and point to other words that rhyme with them.

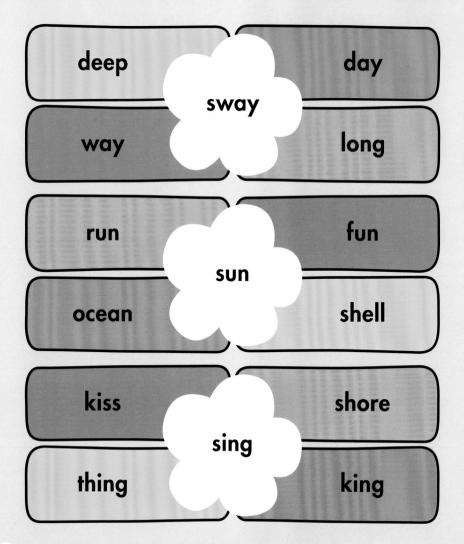

deep

day

sway

way

long

run

fun

sun

ocean

shell

kiss

shore

sing

thing

king

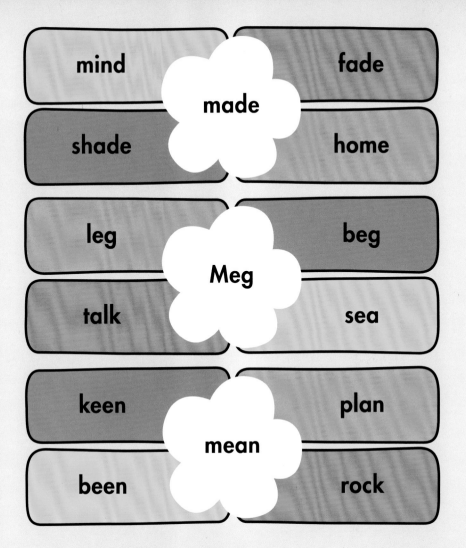

mind	**made**	fade
shade		home

leg	**Meg**	beg
talk		sea

keen		plan
been	**mean**	rock

Now choose a word and make up a rhyming chant.

It is **fun** to **run** in the **sun**.

Sight words

Many common words can be difficult to sound out. Practise them by reading these sentences about the story. Now make more sentences using other sight words from around the border.

Sunshine lived **under** the sea.

The prince's boat was sinking.

Sunshine **told** Meg her wish.

Sunshine's **green** tail became legs.

• boat • sea • call • some • wish • in • sun • before

Sunshine's voice was **in** Meg's shell.

The prince had seen Sunshine **before**.

Meg called **to** the prince.

When he heard Meg, Sam jumped in the sea.

The shell broke and Sunshine got **her** voice back.

Sunshine and the prince **were** married.

• was • no • how • sing • long • had • your • want • new

• then • were • one • her • me • a • all • from

Picture dictionary

Look carefully at the pictures and the words.
Now cover the words, one at a time.
Can you remember how to write them?

bird   **boat**   **mermaid**

potion   **prince**   **shell**

shore   **tail**   **waves**